Little Golden Books

Little Golden Books

Little Golden Books

Little Golden Books

Little Golden Books

A GOLDEN BOOK • NEW YORK

Thomas the Tank Engine & Friends™

CREATED BY BRITT ALLCROFT

Based on the Railway Series by the Reverend W Awdry.
Compilation and cover art © Gullane (Thomas) LLC.
Thomas the Tank Engine & Friends and Thomas & Friends are trademarks of Gullane (Thomas) Limited.
Thomas the Tank Engine & Friends and Design is Reg. U.S. Pat. & Tm. Off.
© HIT Entertainment Limited. All rights reserved.
Published in the United States by Golden Books, an imprint of Random House Children's Books, a division of
Penguin Random House LLC, 1745 Broadway, New York, NY 10019, and in Canada by Random House of Canada,
a division of Penguin Random House Ltd., Toronto. Golden Books, A Golden Book, A Little Golden Book, the
G colophon, and the distinctive gold spine are registered trademarks of Penguin Random House LLC.
The stories contained in this work were originally published separately by Golden Books as follows:
Thomas and the Big, Big Bridge © 2001 Gullane (Thomas) LLC;
Thomas Breaks a Promise © 2006 Gullane (Thomas) LLC;
Thomas and the Great Discovery © 2008 Gullane (Thomas) LLC;
May the Best Engine Win! © 2008 Gullane (Thomas) LLC;
Hero of the Rails © 2010 Gullane (Thomas) LLC;
Misty Island Rescue © 2011 Gullane (Thomas) LLC;
Day of the Diesels © 2012 Gullane (Thomas) LLC;
Blue Mountain Mystery © 2012 Gullane (Thomas) LLC;
King of the Railway © 2013 Gullane (Thomas) LLC.
randomhousekids.com
www.thomasandfriends.com
Educators and librarians, for a variety of teaching tools, visit us at RHTeachersLibrarians.com
ISBN 978-0-385-37644-0
MANUFACTURED IN CHINA
10 9 8 7 6 5 4 3

NINE FAVORITE TALES

Contents

THOMAS
and the
Big, Big
Bridge

Based on The Railway Series
by The Reverend W Awdry

Illustrated by Tom LaPadula and Paul Lopez

It was a special day for the railway!

"We are here to launch the new rail line through the Mountains of Sodor," Sir Topham Hatt announced. "Today we open the big, big bridge!"

What wonderful news! Everyone cheered. The mountains were beautiful. The people of Sodor couldn't wait to visit them.

Everyone wanted to see the big, big bridge. It had towers so high the tops touched the sky. And the valley beneath was so deep that when you were on the big, big bridge, you could barely see the ground.

Thomas was excited about the new rail line.
"This really is a special day!" he said happily.
Then Henry chugged up to Thomas. The big engine frowned.

"I don't want to go to the mountains," Henry said nervously. "It's windy up there—very, very windy." Henry didn't like the wind. Henry didn't like rain or snow or hail, either.

"You're a big engine, Henry!" Thomas said. "You shouldn't be afraid of a little wind."

But Henry was afraid. And that made Thomas a bit afraid, too.

"Gordon! Henry! Thomas! Hitch up your coaches!" called Sir Topham Hatt. "It's time for your first trip to the mountains."

Percy and James were glad they didn't have to go to the mountains. They were afraid to cross the big, big bridge, too.

"There's nothing to be afraid of," Thomas insisted, in a voice loud enough for Percy and James to hear. "It will be easy to cross the big, big bridge."

Thomas and Henry chugged to the platform. Gordon the Express
Engine was already there. His coaches were full of passengers.

Annie and Clarabel were soon hitched behind Thomas. "Hurry,
hurry," they called.

"All aboard!" cried the conductor.

Sir Topham Hatt turned to the crowd and waved his hat one last time.

Toot, toot, Gordon whistled. "Follow me!"

In a burst of steam, the big blue engine was off.

Soon the trains were rolling through the countryside in a long line. Gordon took the lead. Behind him chugged Henry. Then, because he was the smallest, came Thomas.

All along the way, people came out of their houses and cheered when they saw the trains go by.

At the foot of the mountain, Henry slowed to a crawl. "These mountains are much too high," he moaned. "I *can't* go. I'm afraid of heights!"

"Don't be silly," said Thomas bravely. "I'll be right here behind you."

But Henry didn't budge. He was very nervous. And that made Thomas nervous, too.

"Come on!" Thomas gently pushed Henry. "We have to go!"

The brand-new tracks were smooth and shiny, but Henry barely moved along them. The truth was, Henry didn't want to reach the top of the mountain, because then he'd have to cross the big, big bridge.

"If Percy and James and Henry are all afraid," thought Thomas, "maybe *I* should be frightened, too!"

The tracks grew steep as Thomas and Henry puffed up the mountain. They could hardly keep up with Gordon. The big blue engine rushed ahead.

Gordon was a strong engine. The steep tracks didn't tire him at all!

"Wait for us!" Henry called. But Gordon climbed higher and higher, until he was out of sight.

"I don't think I can make it," Henry groaned, his steam giving out at last. "This mountain is too steep!"

"Keep going!" Thomas urged him. "We can't let a little mountain stop us."

But Thomas was having trouble chugging up the steep mountain, too. And he was beginning to worry about crossing the big, big bridge.

Finally, Thomas and Henry arrived at the top of the mountain.
There it was—the big, big bridge! And it was high. It was windy
up there, too—*very* windy.

"I won't go," Henry declared.

"But we have to cross!" Thomas said bravely. "Our passengers want to see the mountains on the other side."

"Hurry, hurry!" Annie and Clarabel cried. The coaches were so excited that Thomas had trouble keeping them in line.

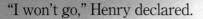

Thomas searched the tracks ahead. Gordon was nowhere to be seen. He had already crossed the bridge and rolled into the mountains beyond.

Thomas and Henry were alone.

"I'll go first," Thomas said at last. "Then you can follow me, Henry."

"If the wind blows, close your eyes," Henry said. "That way you won't see anything scary."

Click-clack! Click-clack! Click-clack! Thomas began to cross the bridge.

Thomas looked up. He could see cottony clouds touching the top of the bridge.

Nervously, he looked down. But the bridge was so high he couldn't see the ground.

A sudden gust of wind shook the bridge. This scared Thomas,
and he closed his eyes so tightly that he couldn't see where he was
going.

Click-clack! Click-clack! Click-CRASH! Thomas came to a sudden
stop. He opened one eye for a quick peek. "Oh, no!" he cried. His
wheels were off the track!

"Are you all right, Thomas?" called Henry.

"I'm stuck," Thomas said glumly. "I couldn't see where I was going and my front wheels have jumped the track."

Just then, Gordon returned. He frowned when he saw Thomas stuck in the middle of the bridge.

26

"Go find Harold," Gordon called to Henry. Relieved, Henry backed
down the mountain to find the helicopter.

Thomas kept his eyes closed. He was too afraid to look. But
inside his coaches, the passengers enjoyed the wonderful view.

Finally, Thomas heard the whirl of rotors. Harold was here to rescue him!

Slowly, Thomas opened his eyes. He looked at the blue sky above and the green mountains all around.

"What a lovely view!" he exclaimed. "I was silly to shut my eyes. I almost missed everything."

"Hitch the rope to your buffer and hold on!" Harold cried.

In no time at all, Harold had lifted Thomas back onto the tracks.
Thomas backed up to where Henry waited.

"Come on, Henry," said Thomas. "The view is spectacular.
I should never have been afraid."

With that, Thomas turned and chugged happily across the big,
big bridge. Henry watched in wonder.

"If *he's* not afraid, maybe I shouldn't be, either!" Henry decided.

Slowly, the big green engine made his way across the bridge, too.

Soon Thomas and Henry arrived at the station house. The
mountains were really lovely. Everyone was happy to have seen them.
But Thomas was the happiest one of all.

He was proud that he had crossed the big, big bridge!

Thomas
Breaks a Promise

Based on The Railway Series
by The Reverend W Awdry

Illustrated by Richard Courtney

The seasons were changing on the Island of Sodor. The leaves had begun to change color, and the air was growing crisp. Thomas the Tank Engine was feeling restless.

"Summer is almost over, and I haven't had any real fun," he complained.

"You're a fussy little engine," replied Gordon. "We're not here to have fun. We're here to work."

Well, that didn't make Thomas feel any better.

"I'd rather be fussy and fun than bossy and boring!" he retorted.

The next morning, Sir Topham Hatt called the engines together.

"We're opening a new branch line tomorrow," he told them. "I need one of you to check the signals on the new line to see that they're all working properly. Who will volunteer?"

"I will," Thomas piped up. "I promise to check very carefully." Checking signals wasn't much fun, but it was better than being bossed around in the train yard.

"Off you go, then," said Sir Topham Hatt. "And be sure to check every signal, Thomas. Safety is our first concern."

Something about shiny new tracks always put Thomas in a good mood. He whistled merrily as he rolled along the new branch line. "Checking signals is really useful," he thought. "Safety is our first concern."

Each time he saw a signal, Thomas made sure that the
arm was in the right position. He also checked to see that the
signal lamp was working, so it could be seen at night.

If the signal arm was down and the lamp was red,
that meant danger on the tracks ahead.
There were hidden junctions . . .

. . . hanging rocks . . .

. . . dangerous curves . . .

. . . and steep hills.

Thomas had almost reached the end of the new branch line when he saw the sign for a carnival. There was nothing Thomas loved more than a carnival. Oh, how he would love to go!

"If I hurry to the carnival now, I can check the rest of the signals later," he told himself. And with that, Thomas turned off and headed into the countryside.

The carnival was splendid. There were games and rides and cotton candy. And there were lots of children.

"Look, it's Thomas!" they cried, and ran to greet their favorite blue engine.

When Thomas got back to the train yard, Sir Topham Hatt was waiting.

"You've been gone a long time, Thomas," he said. "You must have done a very thorough job of checking the signals on the new branch line."

"Yes, sir," peeped Thomas. But suddenly he realized that he'd forgotten to go back and finish the job. He had broken his promise! But how could he tell that to Sir Topham Hatt?

"Good." Sir Topham Hatt beamed. "Then everything is ready for tomorrow's grand opening."

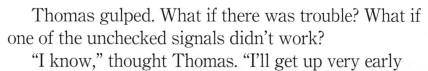

Thomas gulped. What if there was trouble? What if one of the unchecked signals didn't work?

"I know," thought Thomas. "I'll get up very early tomorrow and go out to check the rest of the signals before the grand opening."

That night, Percy was being loaded for his mail run
when a call came into the station. Rain had washed out
a section of track on the mail route. Percy would have to
find a way around.

"Don't worry, Percy." Sir Topham Hatt smiled. "You
can take the new branch line."

Off Percy went, pulling two big cars loaded with mail.

The rain fell heavily. Each time Percy saw a red signal lamp, he slowed carefully until he had passed the dangerous spot. Then suddenly, in the dark, Percy passed another signal. The lamp was not lit, so he didn't see it until too late. The arm was down, for danger! Percy slammed on his brakes, but the rain made the tracks slippery. And there it was ahead—a *very* dangerous curve.

"Oh, no!" cried Percy. He closed his eyes and did his best to hold on through the turn.

CRASH! One of the mail cars flew off the tracks and was smashed to bits. Percy shivered with fear from his close call.

The next morning, Thomas awoke and sneaked out of his shed. Then he saw Percy returning with Sir Topham Hatt.

"Percy has had a terrible fright," Sir Topham said sternly. "He almost derailed because of a signal lamp that didn't work. How could such a thing have happened, Thomas?"

"Oh, sir! I'm so sorry, sir," Thomas sputtered. And it all came rushing out—about the carnival, and the children, and about how he'd forgotten to go back and finish the job.

"I'm sorry I broke my promise, sir," said Thomas sheepishly. "I just wanted to be part of the fun, and then I forgot."

"There will be no fun for you for quite some time," Sir Topham Hatt scolded. "Percy will run your branch line until you've gone and checked every signal on my railway—twice!"

And now, every time Thomas passes a signal, he checks it twice, just to be safe.

Gordon likes to tease him. "Fussy little Thomas certainly is fussy about signals."

"Peep, peep!" says Thomas. "Safety is our first concern."

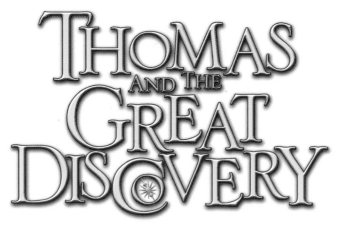

THOMAS AND THE GREAT DISCOVERY

Based on The Railway Series
by The Reverend W Awdry

Illustrated by Tommy Stubbs

It was a beautiful day on the Island of Sodor. Thomas was high in the hills, bringing some freight cars to the wharf. At an unfamiliar junction, he saw an old, overgrown track that looked like a shortcut.

Soon he was rattling down the steep track.
    "No one has been down here for a very long time!"
he huffed.
    Then Thomas gasped. "Fizzling fireboxes!"

He had arrived at a station. It, too, was overgrown, rusty, and very old. There were crumbling platforms, and the station building was covered in ivy. Thomas had never seen such an amazing sight!

"What a funny place to have a station!" he peeped, and looked around some more.

"There are so many buildings. It looks like an old town!" he cried. "I cannot wait to tell everyone about this!"

So Thomas bumped and bashed along the old track and finally made his way down to the wharf.

The next day, the news of Thomas' discovery was all over Sodor. Sir Topham Hatt wanted to visit the hidden town at once.

"Thomas, you have made a wonderful discovery. This was the town of Great Waterton! When steam engines first came to Sodor," Sir Topham Hatt said, "this was an important town. It was called Great Waterton because the springs here provided water for everyone on the island."

"Why does no one live here now?" puffed Thomas.

"The springs ran dry, and the people left to live in new towns. The maps were lost. Everyone thought the town of Great Waterton was lost forever, too."

"But now it is found!" cheered Thomas.

"And if we work hard," added Sir Topham Hatt, "we can have the rededication of the town on Sodor Day!"

In no time, all of Sodor was working hard to fix up Great Waterton. Because Thomas had rediscovered the town, Sir Topham Hatt put him in charge of all the repair work. It was also Thomas' responsibility to explore all the old tracks around Great Waterton. Thomas liked checking old lines, and he liked being in charge. He wanted to show everyone he could do everything.

But one day there was trouble! Thomas was puffing too fast and the track was too old. He toppled off the track. Harvey came to lift him back on, but Thomas was bumped and bruised and had to go to the Works.

While Thomas was at the Works, a friendly new engine named Stanley was put in charge of the work at Great Waterton.

When Thomas was as good as new, he hurried back to Great Waterton. A lot had changed.

Sir Topham Hatt met Thomas. "Stanley has done a good job, so I have decided that Stanley will stay in charge and you will help him."

Thomas' funnel flattened! He had lost the most important job of all.

The next day, Stanley asked Thomas to shunt some
freight cars. Thomas was very good at shunting freight
cars. And he really liked doing it. But he didn't like Stanley
telling him what to do.

Still, he wanted to show how Really Useful he was, so
he shunted freight cars all over Great Waterton. Then he
remembered seeing an old freight car stuck in front of the
abandoned Morgan's Mine. "I'll bring that last one in and Sir
Topham Hatt will give me my old job back." Thomas smiled.

At last, Thomas found the old freight car, and he buffered
up. But he biffed the car too hard. It rolled forward and
disappeared into the mine!

"Cinders and ashes!" exclaimed Thomas. "Where did it go?"
He moved ahead and peered inside.

"I must finish the job!" he huffed. "I'll soon find that freight
car." And Thomas puffed into the mine. . . .

It was very dark. Thomas was happy he had a bright lamp! He looked ahead and saw the freight car rolling away down a slope. Then it disappeared around a bend.

"Bust my buffers!" puffed Thomas. "I'd better go after it!"

Thomas whizzed down the steep slope. "Whee!" he whistled, and "Whoaaa!" he cried. It was scary, but it was also very exciting! Thomas had almost caught up to the freight car.

"You won't get away from me!" he whistled happily.

But Thomas didn't notice the junction ahead! The freight car whizzed to the right. But Thomas sped to the left . . . and saw that the tunnel ahead was blocked!

"Oh, no!" cried Thomas, and he crashed straight through the blocked tunnel and jumped the track! Now Thomas was deep in the mine in a dark tunnel. To top it all off, his fire had gone out! His boiler would soon grow cold. And there was no one around to hear his whistle.

The next morning, Stanley and the other engines arrived for work.

"Where's Thomas?" Stanley asked.

The engines looked around—Thomas wasn't there.

Thomas was missing!

It was the biggest calamity Sodor had ever known!

Everyone looked for Thomas. They checked the quarries.

They searched the docks.

They toured
every town.

They scoured every hill and hunted
in every valley. But Thomas was
nowhere to be found!

And then Stanley had a thought. "Maybe Thomas is up on the forgotten tracks around Great Waterton. I'll look for him there."

When Stanley was high up in the hills, he whistled and whistled. "Where are you, Thomas?" But only his echo came back.

Stanley looked everywhere. Then he spotted Morgan's Mine. "Could Thomas have gone into the mine?" Stanley wondered. He whistled one last time . . . and this time, Thomas heard him.

"It's Stanley!" he gasped.

With his very last puff . . . and his very last huff . . . Thomas blew his whistle as loudly as he could . . .

. . . and Stanley heard him! He slowly entered the dark mine. "Thomas!" he whistled happily. "Is that you?"

Thomas had run out of puff. He couldn't whistle again. He could only wait and hope that Stanley would find him.

It wasn't long before Thomas heard Stanley chuffing up behind him.

"Stanley!" he peeped. "I'm very happy that you are here!"

"Thomas!" whistled Stanley. "I'm very happy to find you. Where have you been?"

"I was trying to be a Really Useful engine," tooted Thomas.

"Don't worry, Thomas," Stanley chuffed. "I'll have you back on the track in no time!"

Soon Stanley was coupled up to Thomas. He pulled and tugged. Thomas was heavy, but Stanley didn't give up.

"I can do it!" Stanley wheeshed, and with a mighty heave, he pulled his friend back onto the track.

"Hooray!" tooted Thomas.

Then there was a very loud crack! The valve in Stanley's boiler had burst! Stanley was a strong engine . . . but pulling Thomas had been too much. Now Stanley couldn't move!

"Don't worry!" whistled Thomas. "It's my turn to help you! With your coal, I can push you home."

Stanley smiled.

In no time at all, Thomas' boiler was bubbling and his steam was wheeshing. Thomas found an open siding, got behind Stanley, and started to push.

"Here we go, Stanley!" Thomas huffed happily.

Stanley smiled back. And puff by puff, Thomas pushed
Stanley up and out of the mine. The old tracks rattled and
creaked, but Thomas didn't mind. He was happy and proud
to push his new friend Stanley home.

At last, Thomas and Stanley pulled into Great Waterton junction. Thomas was tired, but he had never felt happier!

When the other engines saw Thomas and Stanley, they tooted and whistled, and soon the sound of engine whistles echoed all around Great Waterton.

The news quickly spread throughout Sodor! "Thomas has been found!" the engines whistled.

Sir Topham Hatt grandly proclaimed, "Stanley saved Thomas, and Thomas saved Stanley!"

For the next couple of days, everyone worked hard to get Great Waterton ready for Sodor Day. Now Thomas was happy that Stanley had come to Sodor. Thomas had a wonderful new friend.

And just in time, everything was done.

The weather for Sodor Day was perfect! Sir Topham Hatt arrived and beamed. "Well done to you all! This is the grandest Sodor Day ever!" He and Lady Hatt stood beside the red ribbon with a great big pair of scissors.

"Thanks to Thomas, Great Waterton is no longer lost! And thanks to Stanley, the work was finished Right On Time. Welcome to the town of Great Waterton!" boomed Sir Topham Hatt.

Lady Hatt snipped the ribbon.

"We're all Really Useful Engines," puffed Thomas happily. He couldn't have been prouder!

May the Best Engine Win!

Based on The Railway Series
by The Reverend W Awdry

Illustrated by Tommy Stubbs

Early one morning on the Island of Sodor, Sir Topham Hatt came to the Yard. Thomas and Emily were preparing for a busy day.

Thomas always worked very hard. He was proud to be a Really Useful Engine.

Emily was new. She wanted to prove that she was Really Useful, too. She hoped that Sir Topham Hatt would see how excited she was to start the day.

"Thomas, there's a lot to do today. I hope that everything gets done on time," said Sir Topham Hatt.

"Why should Thomas get all the work?" asked Emily. "I can do anything he can. I'm faster than him, too!"

Sir Topham Hatt was glad that Emily wanted to help. He told them, "I can divide up the duties so that both of you will have the same workload today."

Emily knew it would be a long day, but she smiled. She told Thomas, "Now you'll see what I can do."

Thomas was used to long days. "Emily, this might be too much work for you," he teased. "You should let me do more."

"*Pfffft!*" she puffed. "I'll race you! Whoever finishes and makes it back to the station first is the winner."

"Let's go!" peeped Thomas.

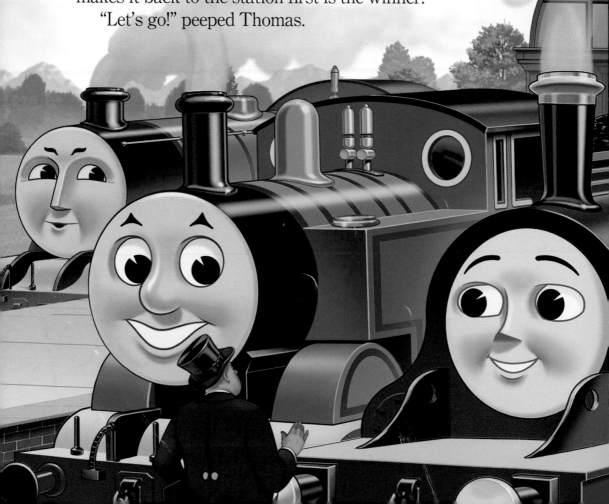

With a *Peep!* and a *Poop!*, Thomas and Emily left
the station side by side.

Emily's first stop was the Quarry. She'd brought crates full of new tools, and she had to stay in place while the workers unloaded them. After all the crates were taken away, the workers hitched her to freight cars full of large stones.

Emily knew that Really Useful Engines were supposed to be good at waiting. But it was difficult for her to be patient.

"Please hurry," she told the workers. "I don't want Thomas to get ahead!"

While Emily was at the Quarry, Thomas was running his Branch Line.

He moved from station to station. At every stop, more passengers got off and Annie and Clarabel got lighter and lighter.

"I'll bet I'm pulling ahead of Emily already," thought Thomas.

Along the way to his last station, Thomas saw Emily. She was going to Suddery with stone from the Quarry.

"There you are, slowcoach!" she called.

Thomas laughed. "That stone looks awfully heavy!" he said.

He hoped that Emily would get tired from hauling such a heavy load.

Thomas' second job was to deliver a load of barrels to the docks. He had to wait for the barrels to be moved onto boats.

Thomas was not a very patient engine, but he knew it would do no good to win the race if he didn't do his job just right.

"The other engines will tease me forever if Emily wins," he thought. He would have to go extra fast to his next stop.

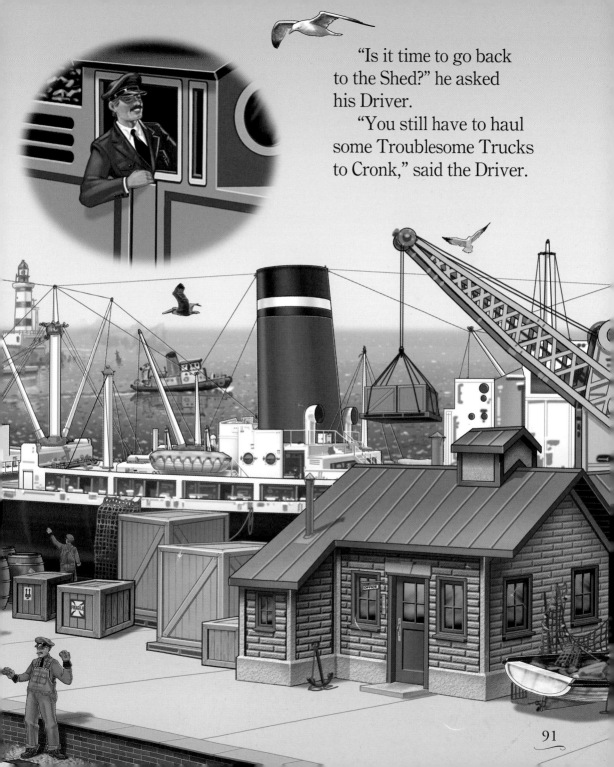

"Is it time to go back to the Shed?" he asked his Driver.

"You still have to haul some Troublesome Trucks to Cronk," said the Driver.

Troublesome Trucks were always
bumping and bashing. Thomas had
to work hard to keep them in line.
"Don't try anything funny!"
he said as they left the station.

But soon Thomas had to stop at a signal.

The Signalman explained, "Some rocks have fallen onto the tracks. You'll have to wait until the way is clear."

"Oh, bother," said Thomas. "I wonder where Emily is now."

Emily had left Suddery. Her final job was a Special along the mountain route.

On the way, she passed Thomas, who was stopped at the signal.

"Poor Thomas!" she called to him. "Looks like you're stuck!"

Emily sped up.

She saw a sign warning of a winding track ahead,
but she didn't want to slow down and risk losing
the race.

The track was difficult, and she was going too fast.
Her Driver told her to slow down.

But it was too late. As Emily took a turn, one of her trucks tipped over!

Now she had to wait for help. "Thomas will get ahead for sure," she thought.

Thomas was having better luck. The rocks had been
cleared, and he was almost done with his last job of
the day.

He saw Harvey moving on the opposite track. "Hello,
Harvey," he peeped. "Where are you headed?"

"Emily's hit a spot of trouble up the line," said
Harvey. "Nothing to worry about."

Emily was glad to see Harvey. She thanked him for his help.

"I'll take the rest of the path slowly," she said. "If I'm more careful, I still might beat Thomas."

Thomas was having some difficulty with the Troublesome Trucks. They made him go faster than he wanted to. But his brakes were strong and he was able to stay on the track.

Once the Troublesome Trucks were unhitched, he sped away toward home. "I hope Emily isn't there yet," he thought.

The sun was nearly setting by the time Thomas arrived at the Yard.

He didn't see Emily anywhere.

Emily arrived only a minute later. When she saw
Thomas, she frowned. She had really wanted to beat him.

Thomas saw her sad expression. He knew that *he* would
have been sad if he had lost, so he decided not to brag.

"That was a close race," he said.

"You won fair and square," said Emily.

"But I'll beat you tomorrow," she added.
Thomas laughed. "We'll see about that!"

Based on The Railway Series
by The Reverend W Awdry

Illustrated by Tommy Stubbs

Thomas was enjoying a quiet summer day . . .
until Spencer raced by with a *whoosh!*
  Spencer was visiting Sodor to help build
a summer house for the Duke and Duchess
of Boxford.

Spencer thought he was better and faster than all the other engines, so Thomas challenged him to a race.

Ready, set, GO!

Thomas and Spencer sped along the rails and raced around Sodor. Up and down hills, faster and faster they went.

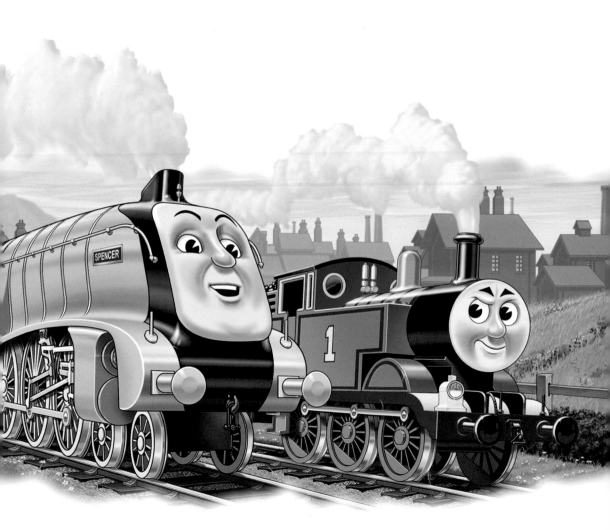

Suddenly, Thomas' brakes broke! He crashed through some bushes—and made an incredible discovery.

Thomas found an old engine in need of repair. The engine's name was Hiro, and he had come from a distant island a long time ago. Hiro was once called the Master of the Railway.

Hiro was afraid he'd be sent to the scrap yard because he wasn't Really Useful anymore. Thomas promised to repair him in secret and make him as good as new.

Thomas found some spare parts at the bustling Sodor Steamworks. "These will help Hiro," he peeped excitedly.

But as he was on his way to visit Hiro, Thomas learned something terrible.

"The Duke and Duchess of Boxford's summer house is right next to Hiro's hiding place," Thomas peeped. "Spencer will be here every day!"

Thomas knew he would have to be careful, or Spencer would discover Hiro.

Just then, Spencer steamed around the bend. "I think you're up to something sneaky," he puffed. Thomas didn't answer. He just chuffed away nervously.

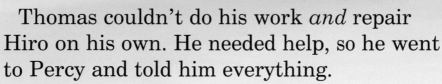

Thomas couldn't do his work *and* repair
Hiro on his own. He needed help, so he went
to Percy and told him everything.

"Of course I'll help," Percy peeped. "What
can I do?"

So Percy hid his mail cars and helped Thomas with his work. But the loads were too heavy for Percy. He soon popped a valve and needed to be repaired at the Steamworks.

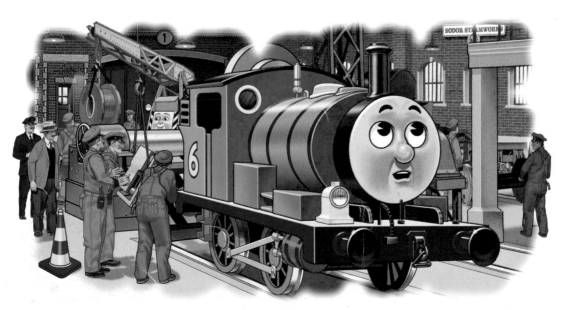

Sir Topham Hatt was very cross that Percy was doing Thomas' work. Thomas didn't tell Sir Topham Hatt about Hiro. But he did tell the other engines, because he knew he needed their help, too.

Spencer wanted to know Thomas' secret, so he followed him everywhere. Thomas made sure to lead Spencer as far from Hiro as possible.

He even went out to the Quarry, where Spencer had a dusty accident.

Meanwhile, all the other engines helped Hiro. They were amazed by his stories about his distant home. Hiro liked his new friends, but he missed his old friends.

A few days later, Hiro was almost as good
as new. He just needed Percy to bring one
last part. But while Hiro and Thomas waited,
Spencer huffed along the track.

"I knew you were up to something sneaky!"
Spencer puffed.

Hiro tried to race away. But without his last part, he sputtered to a stop.

As Spencer chuffed off, he laughed and said he would tell Sir Topham Hatt that the pile of scrap metal was ready for the smelting yard.

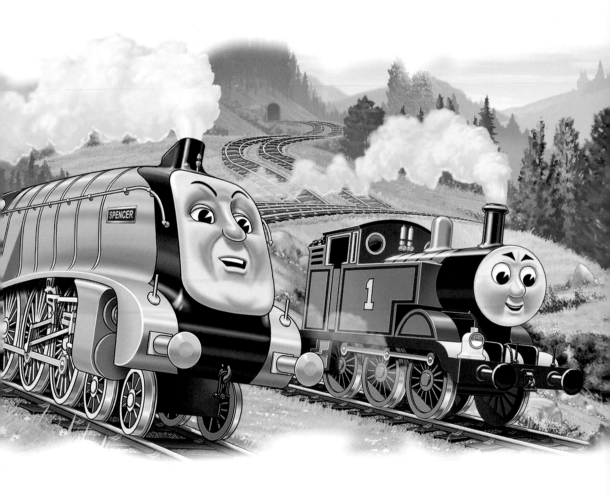

Thomas knew he had to get to Sir Topham
Hatt first. He and Spencer roared through
tunnels and rushed around bends. It was the
race of their lives!

Spencer was too heavy for the old track that crossed the marsh. With a creak and a crash, he splashed into the water.

Thomas sped to Knapford Station and told Sir Topham Hatt everything.

"You have found the Master of the Railway? We must help Hiro at once!" Sir Topham Hatt exclaimed.

After a visit to the Sodor Steamworks, Hiro was as good as new!

Thomas and Percy couldn't believe their eyes. They blew their whistles happily.

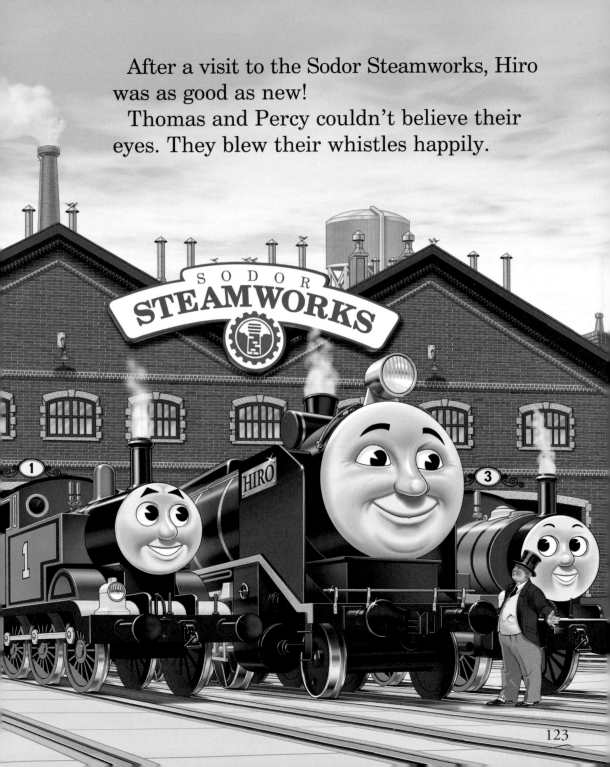

Later, Rocky, Thomas, and Hiro pulled Spencer from the mud. But only Hiro was mighty enough to pull Spencer all the way back to the Steamworks. Spencer said he was sorry for being so mean to everyone.

Spencer, Thomas, and Hiro finished
the Duke and Duchess' summer house
together. Hiro liked his friends on Sodor,
but he was still feeling very homesick.
Thomas knew Sir Topham Hatt could help.

It was time for Hiro to go home. All the engines gathered at Brendam Docks to say goodbye to their friend—the Master of the Railway.

Misty Island
RESCUE

Based on The Railway Series
by The Reverend W Awdry

Illustrated by Tommy Stubbs

Thomas and Percy were helping to build a new Search and Rescue Center on the Island of Sodor. There was much work to do.

"It will be made of the strongest wood of all—
jobi wood," said Sir Topham Hatt. "The wood
will arrive today at Brendam Docks."

Diesel tried to move the logs by himself and had a terrible accident. Luckily, Thomas saved Diesel—but the logs fell into the sea.

Sir Topham Hatt was proud of Thomas. He asked Thomas to travel to the Mainland and bring back more jobi wood. Percy was worried that the trip would be dangerous.

A steamboat pulled Thomas on a raft toward the Mainland. Far out at sea, Thomas heard a loud crack.

"Fizzling fireboxes!" he peeped. "The chain to the steamboat has snapped!"

The next morning, Thomas found himself on a strange island. It was very misty. He peeped hello, but nobody answered. So he went exploring.

Suddenly, Thomas came fender to fender
with three strange engines. Their names were
Bash, Dash, and Ferdinand, and they called
themselves the Logging Locos. Bash told
Thomas he was on Misty Island.

Meanwhile, everyone on Sodor was looking for Thomas. Sir Topham Hatt and Captain raced out to sea.

Percy searched every track. Harold took to the sky.

Back on Misty Island, Bash, Dash, and
Ferdinand showed Thomas where they lived.
It was an old logging camp filled with winding
tracks and rickety cabins.

Thomas made an amazing discovery. "This camp is filled with jobi wood!" he peeped. "That's the wood we need to build the Search and Rescue Center!"

Thomas told the Logging Locos all about the Rescue Center. They agreed to help him collect the logs.

But the Logging Locos didn't like working.
They just wanted to play games and bounce
on Shake Shake Bridge. Thomas definitely did
not like the wibbly, wobbly bridge.

Ol' Wheezy, the giant log loader, wasn't much help, either. He liked to throw logs, not stack them.

After much biffing and bashing, Thomas had flatbeds full of jobi logs, but he didn't know how to get back to Sodor.

Bash told him about an old tunnel that connected Misty Island to Sodor.

Pushing their flatbeds full of logs, the engines
reached the old tunnel. It was cold and dark.
The Logging Locos were scared.

"Don't worry," peeped Thomas. "With a whir
and a whiff, we'll be on the Island of Sodor."

Suddenly, with a rumble and a crash, there was a cave-in! Rocks tumbled down around the engines. They were trapped—and no one knew where they were!

Thomas saw a hole in the roof of the tunnel.
He sent up puffs of steam.
Thomas hoped someone would
see the puffs and come to
the rescue.

Somebody did see the steam puffs—Percy!
"It's Thomas," Percy peeped excitedly. "He's on
Misty Island, and he needs help!"

Whiff told Percy about an old tunnel that led to Misty Island. Percy knew it would be dangerous, but it was the fastest way to save Thomas.

Percy raced through the tunnel. It was dark and twisty. At last he found the cave-in. "Watch out, Thomas!" Percy puffed. "I'm going to push back the rocks!"

Percy rocked and rolled and pumped his pistons.
CRASH!
Percy broke through the boulders. Thomas and
the Logging Locos were saved.

Sir Topham Hatt was very happy that
Thomas and his new friends were safe. And
with all the new jobi wood, the Rescue Center
would be finished very soon.

"Today is a special day made possible by very special engines," Sir Topham Hatt said at the opening of the Search and Rescue Center. The people cheered. The engines all peeped. Thomas' pistons pumped with pride.

Based on The Railway Series
by The Reverend W Awdry

Illustrated by Tommy Stubbs

One beautiful morning on the Island of Sodor,
Thomas and Percy were enjoying a ride in the
country. Suddenly, they saw black smoke in the sky.
They raced to find out what was the matter.

An old farm shed was on fire! Percy and
Thomas let firefighters take buckets of water
from their tanks to put out the blaze, but it
was slow work. Luckily, a new engine named
Belle arrived. She shot water from two spouts
on her tanks. The flames fizzled out.

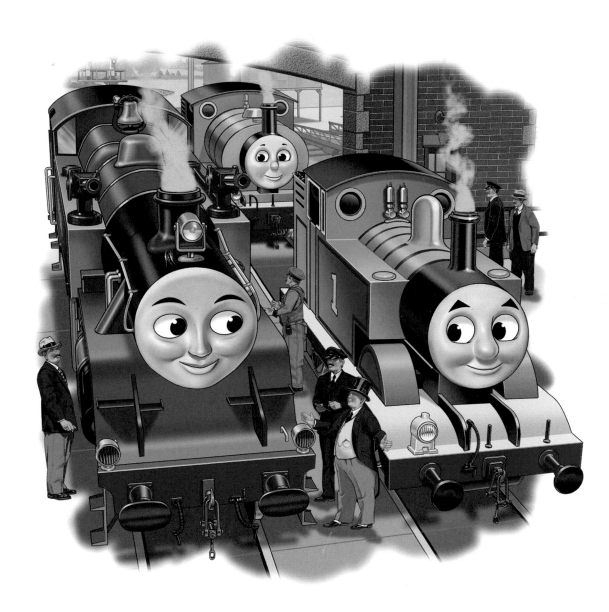

Back at the Steamworks, everyone cheered for Belle. "Thank you," she peeped. "But I'm not a real fire engine. You need Flynn the Fire Engine. He's fast and fearless. He's a real hero."

The next day, Thomas took Belle on a tour of the Island of Sodor. They forgot to invite Percy. He felt left out and very alone.

Diesel oiled up next to Percy. He invited Percy
to visit the Dieselworks. "You'll be our special
guest," he hissed.

Steamies didn't usually go to the Dieselworks,
but Percy wanted friends who had time for him.
He wanted to be a special guest.

Percy enjoyed his visit. All the Diesels were very friendly, but the building was dingy, old, and dirty. They didn't even have a crane!

"You need a new Dieselworks," Percy said
to Diesel 10. "I will ask Thomas to tell Sir
Topham Hatt. He always listens to Thomas."
Diesel 10 liked this idea.

Percy raced back to the Steamworks to tell
Thomas about his adventure, but Thomas was too
busy to listen. Flynn the Fire Engine had arrived,
and Thomas was showing him around Sodor.

That night, Percy saw something that really troubled him—Flynn was in Percy's berth at Tidmouth Sheds! Percy decided not to stay where he wasn't wanted.

Percy puffed to the Dieselworks. He brought Kevin because he knew the Diesels didn't have a crane.

"We'll both be needed at the Dieselworks," Percy peeped.

The next morning, Percy told the Steamies where
he had been all night. Everyone was amazed.

Percy asked Thomas if he could help the Diesels get
a new Dieselworks. They chugged off together to talk
to Diesel 10.

But Diesel 10 no longer wanted Thomas' help.

"We're going to take over the Steamworks," said Diesel 10. "We want you to lead us, Percy!"

Percy felt grander than Gordon! He and the Diesels rolled away, leaving behind a very angry Thomas.

But when they reached the Steamworks, the Diesels wouldn't listen to Percy.

"The Steamworks is ours!" Diesel 10 roared. "And we're not giving it back!"

To make matters worse, Percy discovered that Thomas was being held prisoner at the Dieselworks!

Percy hurried to help Thomas. As he
screeched to a stop, sparks flew from his
wheels. Some oily rags caught fire, and
flames spread across the Dieselworks!

Percy knew he needed Flynn's help. He found
the bold red engine, and together they rushed
back to the Dieselworks. Flynn put out the fire
while Percy saved Thomas.

Percy and Thomas then raced to the Steamworks to stop the Diesels. As they rolled along, they collected their friends—Belle, Edward, Henry, Gordon, James, Toby, and Emily.

They all knew that friends are strongest when they stick together.

The Diesels were surprised to see the Steamies, but they refused to leave the Steamworks—until Sir Topham Hatt arrived. He was very cross.

"Diesel 10," he said sternly. "You have caused confusion and delay on my railway!

"It was always my plan to build a new Dieselworks," Sir Topham Hatt explained. "But everything takes time. Now the Diesels and the Steamies must work together to build a new Dieselworks."

Soon the new Dieselworks was finished! At the grand opening, the Diesels beamed and the Steamies peeped proudly. Everyone was happy, especially Percy and Thomas. They were best friends again!

Based on The Railway Series
by The Reverend W Awdry

Illustrated by Tommy Stubbs

It was a busy day at the Blue Mountain Quarry. Rusty shunted trucks of slate. Owen lifted equipment up and down the rocky walls.

The Narrow Gauge quarry engines were smaller and lighter than the other engines. They had special tracks.

Paxton, a visiting Diesel, was impressed by how hard they all worked.

Suddenly, there was a loud noise. Giant
stones were falling from Blondin Bridge!
Rheneas tried to stop, but his heavy trucks
pushed him toward the bridge.

Rheneas rolled
across the bridge
just in time!

Unfortunately, Paxton
was buried under
some fallen stones.
He was all right,
but he needed
repairs.

Thomas went to the quarry to work in Paxton's place. "I like working with my Narrow Gauge friends," he whistled. Suddenly, a small green engine darted out of a tunnel.

"Hello!" peeped Thomas.

But the little green engine rolled away into another tunnel.

Thomas asked Skarloey about the green engine.
"His name is Luke. He hides here because he
did something very bad."
Thomas promised to keep the secret locked
in his funnel.

"What did Luke do that was so bad?" Thomas
wondered aloud later that night. "Don't worry,
Luke. I'll find a way to help you."

But Thomas wasn't really alone. Someone
was listening.

The next morning as Thomas chuffed to work, Luke emerged from a tunnel.

"Hi, Thomas," Luke said. "I'm sorry I hid from you. Will you be my friend?"

"I'd like that," replied Thomas.

Thomas and Luke worked together at the
boulder drop all day.

"Why do you keep hiding?" Thomas asked
Luke.

They didn't notice that Paxton was back.
He was listening to Luke's story.

"I first came to the Island of Sodor on a boat," said Luke. "When they were lifting me off it, I bumped into a little yellow engine . . . and sent him splashing into the sea!"

Paxton couldn't believe what he had heard! He raced off to tell Diesel.

Later, Thomas heard Paxton telling Diesel the story.

"The yellow engine was never seen again," said Diesel. "We have to tell Sir Topham Hatt and Mr. Percival."

Thomas was worried. He had to find out what happened to that little yellow engine. Thomas chuffed to the Steamworks to ask Victor if he knew anything. "That was me!" said Victor.

Victor's story about his trip to the Island of Sodor was the same as Luke's—except for one important detail.

"My chains were broken!" Victor said. "That's why I fell into the sea. But Cranky fished me out."

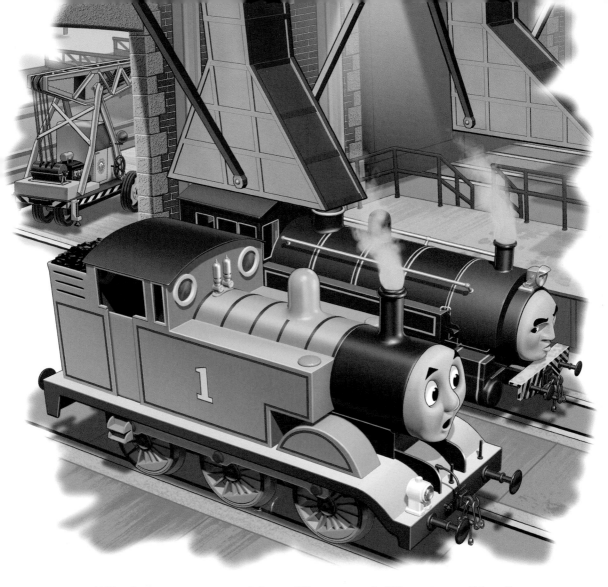

"So it was an accident!" peeped Thomas. "And you were repaired!"

"Yes," replied Victor. "I chose to be painted a new color—red!"

"I'm glad I found you," Thomas said. "Luke needs your help."

Diesel tracked down Luke at the quarry. Luke rolled up the narrow gauge tracks to get away. Diesel couldn't follow.

"You can't hide!" shouted Diesel. "Sir Topham Hatt is going to kick you off Sodor! Thomas can't save you now!"

"Yes, I can!" peeped Thomas.

The quarry walls were high, so Thomas needed Owen's help. Thomas was heavy, but Owen lifted him all the way to the top.

But Thomas' wheels were too big for the narrow gauge tracks! They skidded off the rails—and Thomas rolled toward a cliff! Just then, Luke came around a bend.

"Watch out, Thomas!" cried Diesel. "He's going to push you off! Just like he did to that yellow engine!"

"Don't worry, Thomas," said Luke. "I'll get you back to Owen."

Luke gently pulled Thomas back toward the platform.

"You're doing it!" peeped Thomas. Luke felt strong. He pulled Thomas to Owen, but the two engines weighed too much. The platform began to drop straight down!

Owen worked his hardest. Gears whined. Sparks flew. He stopped the platform before it hit the ground. Thomas and Luke were safe! All the engines cheered, except for Diesel.

Just then, Sir Topham Hatt and Mr. Percival arrived. They were confused and angry.

"Luke is a bad engine!" said Diesel. "He pushed a yellow engine into the sea."

Victor steamed into the quarry. Everyone was surprised.

"Luke, you didn't push me," Victor said. "It was an accident. I was repaired and painted red."

For the first time in a long, long time, Luke was truly happy.

Sir Topham Hatt was upset with Diesel. "You didn't find out the whole story," he said. "What really happened is what really matters."

"Well done, Thomas," said Sir Topham Hatt. "Today is a happy day for Mr. Percival and his engines." Thomas and all his friends, new and old, whistled happily.

KING OF THE RAILWAY

Based on The Railway Series
by The Reverend W Awdry

Illustrated by Tommy Stubbs

One morning, Thomas and Percy were shunting trucks at Brendam Docks. Suddenly, a truck bashed into Percy's buffer and tipped over. A crate fell out and split open.

"Thomas, look!" peeped Percy. "There's a robot!"

"That's not a robot," grumbled Cranky. "It's a suit of armor."

"Cranky's right," said Sir Topham Hatt. "Once, the Island of Sodor was ruled by kings and knights. The greatest king was the beloved King Godred. He wore a golden crown. But the crown went missing long ago!"

An earl was visiting the island. Thomas
delivered the crate to him. There he met Millie,
the earl's Narrow Gauge engine.

"I run the estate railway for the earl," Millie
peeped happily.

"I wish I had King Godred's golden crown,"
said the earl. "Then my plan would be complete."

Thomas' friend Jack the Digger was also working at the estate.

"I'm helping the earl restore the castle," puffed Jack.

"So *that's* his plan!" whistled Thomas.

Thomas, Percy, and James spent the day
happily shunting containers . . . until Thomas
came upon a flatbed with a large crate on it.
The earl said it was a special delivery for the
Steamworks.

At the Steamworks, a gantry crane lifted the crate and revealed an old engine named Stephen. His wood was worn, and he had rust holes in his boiler.

"Surprise!" the old engine peeped.

Victor said he'd have Stephen fixed up
in no time.

"I have a special job for Stephen," said the
earl. "But it's best not to say anything yet."

"I won't," peeped Thomas. "I promise."

Victor worked quickly. Soon Stephen's funnel was straightened and his boiler was fixed. With a fresh coat of paint, he was good as new.

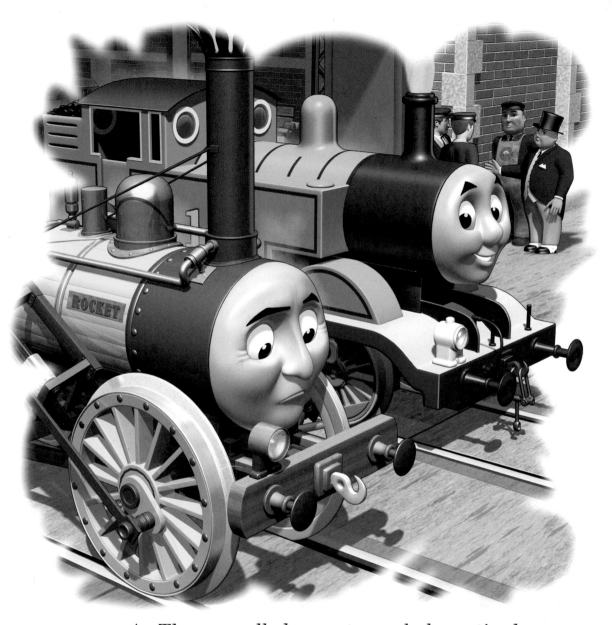

As Thomas rolled away to work, he noticed
that Stephen looked sad.

Thomas told Stephen that the earl had a
special job for him. Stephen was very excited.

Stephen wondered what his special job would be. Victor didn't know, so Stephen rolled down to Brendam Docks.

"There's no work here for an old engine like you," Cranky said.

Stephen wound his way up to the quarry.
"I'm looking for my new job," Stephen said.
"We can always use help," Luke peeped.
But each truck Stephen tried to pull was just
too heavy.

"Once I worked in a mine," said Stephen. "Are there any mines around here?"

"There is an old mine near the castle ruins," said Skarloey.

Stephen found the entrance to the mine,
but it was boarded up. No one had worked
there in years.

Suddenly, some Troublesome Trucks slipped loose and roared down the hill. They were headed right toward Stephen! He had no choice but to push into the mine.

Stephen's funnel struck the roof, and rocks crashed down behind him, sealing up the entrance. He searched for a way out, but the tracks just led him in circles. He only found an old wooden crate.

Thomas and Percy searched for Stephen.
Outside the old mine, Thomas saw something
familiar lying on the ground. It was Stephen's
funnel!

Thomas got Jack the Digger, who started hauling rocks away from the mine entrance. As soon as it was clear, Thomas raced into the dark mine. "Stephen!" he peeped.

Stephen heard Thomas coming his way.
He wanted to call out, but he was too weak.
Finally, Thomas turned a corner, and the
beam from his lamp revealed a welcome sight.

Thomas carefully pushed Stephen out of the dark mine. The earl was there to greet them.

"I found something in the mine," Stephen said. "There's a big wooden chest."

The next day, the earl revealed what was in the crate. It was the king's golden crown! "It is all thanks to Stephen, our castle guide," he said.

Stephen's new funnel glittered just like the crown.